Dear Parents:

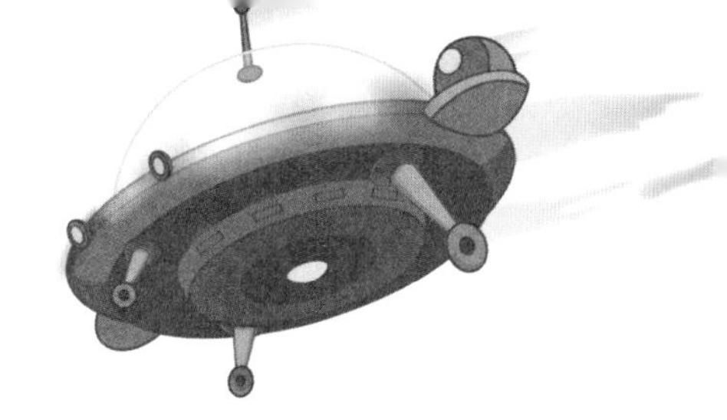

Congratulations! Your child is taking the first steps on an exciting journey. The destination? Independent reading!

STEP INTO READING® will help your child get there. The program offers five steps to reading success. Each step includes fun stories and colorful art or photographs. In addition to original fiction and books with favorite characters, there are Step into Reading Non-Fiction Readers, Phonics Readers and Boxed Sets, Sticker Readers, and Comic Readers—a complete literacy program with something to interest every child.

Learning to Read, Step by Step!

Ready to Read **Preschool–Kindergarten**
• big type and easy words • rhyme and rhythm • picture clues
For children who know the alphabet and are eager to begin reading.

Reading with Help **Preschool–Grade 1**
• basic vocabulary • short sentences • simple stories
For children who recognize familiar words and sound out new words with help.

Reading on Your Own **Grades 1–3**
• engaging characters • easy-to-follow plots • popular topics
For children who are ready to read on their own.

Reading Paragraphs **Grades 2–3**
• challenging vocabulary • short paragraphs • exciting stories
For newly independent readers who read simple sentences with confidence.

Ready for Chapters **Grades 2–4**
• chapters • longer paragraphs • full-color art
For children who want to take the plunge into chapter books but still like colorful pictures.

STEP INTO READING® is designed to give every child a successful reading experience. The grade levels are only guides; children will progress through the steps at their own speed, developing confidence in their reading.

Remember, a lifetime love of reading starts with a single step!

Visit us on the Web!
StepIntoReading.com
randomhousekids.com

Educators and librarians, for a variety of teaching tools, visit us at
RHTeachersLibrarians.com

ISBN 978-0-553-53886-1 (trade) — ISBN 978-0-553-53887-8 (lib. bdg.)

Printed in the United States of America

10 9 8 7

Chase's Space Case

By Kristen L. Depken
Illustrated by MJ Illustrations

Random House New York

Ryder and the pups
are looking
at the stars.
They see a spaceship!

Crash!

A space bubble comes out of the ship.

A cow is trapped
in the space bubble!

Mayor Goodway calls
the PAW Patrol
for help.

Ready for action!

Chase helps the cow.

Then he looks around.

A space alien has put
Mayor Goodway
in a bubble!

Chase helps.
Then he checks the farm
for the alien.

Melon.

Melon.

Space alien.

Melon.

Another bubble!

Zip!

Chase pulls himself free.

The space alien is

in the Lookout!

He is trying
to fly the Lookout home!
He misses his mom.

The spaceship is back!

Rocky fixed it.

The space alien is happy!

The space alien gives Ryder and the pups a ride.

Best ride ever!

Ryder and the pups
wave goodbye
to their new friend.